Farmyard Tales Flip Books

Scarecrow's Secret

Heather Amery

Illustrated by Stephen Cartwright

Language consultant: Betty Root
Series editor: Jenny Tyler

There is a little yellow duck to find on every page.

This is Apple Tree Farm.

This is Mrs. Boot, the farmer. She has two children, called Poppy and Sam, and a dog called Rusty.

Mr. Boot is working in the barn.

"What are you doing, Dad?" asks Sam. "I'm tying lots of straw on these poles," says Mr Boot.

"What is it?"

"You'll soon see," says Mr. Boot. "Go and get my old coat from the shed, please. Bring my old hat too."

"It's going to be a scarecrow."

Poppy and Sam come back with the coat and hat.
Then they help Mr. Boot put them on the scarecrow.

"He's just like a nice old man."

"I've got some old gloves for him," says Sam.
"Let's call him Mr. Straw," says Poppy.

"He's finished now."

"Help me carry him, please, Poppy," says
Mr. Boot. "You bring the spade, Sam."

They all go to the cornfield.

Mr. Boot digs a hole in the field. Then he pushes
in the pole so that Mr. Straw stands up.

"He does look real."

"I'm sure Mr. Straw will scare off all the birds," says Sam. "Especially the crows," says Poppy.

Mr. Straw is doing a good job.

Every day Mr. Boot, Poppy and Sam look at
Mr. Straw. There are no birds in the cornfield.

"There's Farmer Dray's scarecrow."

"He's no good at all," says Sam. "The birds are eating all the corn and standing on the scarecrow."

"Why is Mr. Straw so good?"

"Sometimes he looks as if he is moving," says
Poppy. "His coat goes up and down. It's very odd."

"Let's go and look."

"Let's creep up very quietly," says Sam. And they tiptoe across the cornfield to look at Mr. Straw.

"There's something inside his coat."

"It's moving," says Poppy. "And it's making a funny noise. What is it?" says Sam.

"It's our cat and her kittens."

Carefully they open the coat. There is Whiskers, the cat, and two baby kittens hiding in the straw.

"So that's the scarecrow's secret."

"Whiskers is helping Mr. Straw to frighten off the birds," says Poppy. "Clever Mr. Straw," says Sam.

It is time to go home.

Mrs. Rose waves goodbye. "That was such fun,"
she says. Ears trots home. She has a new hat too.

Ears wins a prize.

"Well done," says the judge, giving her a rosette.
He gives Mrs. Rose a prize too. It is a hat.

Ears pulls the cart into the show ring.

She trots in front of the judges. She stops and goes when Mrs. Rose tells her.

Ears is very good now.

The lady is called Mrs. Rose. She climbs into the cart. "Come on," she says, and shakes the reins.

"Naughty donkey," says Sam.

"I'm sorry," Mrs. Boot says to the lady. "Would you like to take Ears to the best donkey competition?"

Ears runs away.

Mrs. Boot, Poppy and Sam and the lady run
after her and catch her.

"That looks good to eat."

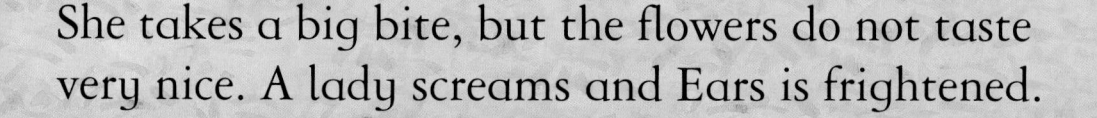

She takes a big bite, but the flowers do not taste very nice. A lady screams and Ears is frightened.

Ears looks for food.

Ears trots across the field to the show ring.
She sees a bunch of flowers and some fruit.

Ears gets free.

Ears is hungry and bored with nothing to do.
She pulls and pulls on the rope until she is free.

"You stay here, Ears."

At the show ground, Mrs. Boot ties Ears to a
fence. "Stay here. We'll be back soon," she says.

Off they go to the Show.

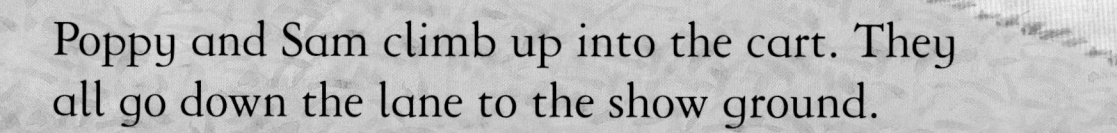

Poppy and Sam climb up into the cart. They
all go down the lane to the show ground.

Ears has a little cart.

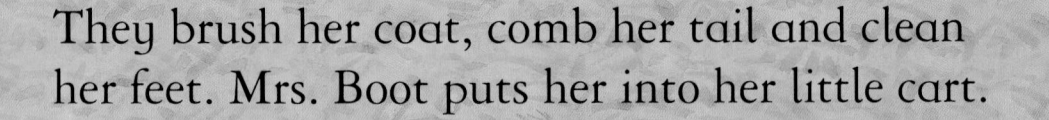

They brush her coat, comb her tail and clean her feet. Mrs. Boot puts her into her little cart.

Ears, the donkey, is going out.

Poppy and Sam catch Ears and take her to the
farmyard. Today is the day of the Show.

There is a donkey on the farm.

The donkey is called Ears. She lives in a field
with lots of grass, but she is always hungry.

This is Apple Tree Farm.

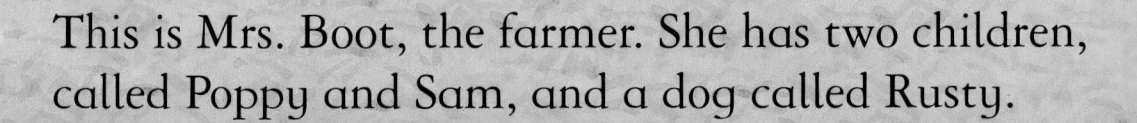

This is Mrs. Boot, the farmer. She has two children, called Poppy and Sam, and a dog called Rusty.

Farmyard Tales Flip Books

The Hungry Donkey

Heather Amery

Illustrated by Stephen Cartwright

Language consultant: Betty Root
Series editor: Jenny Tyler

There is a little yellow duck to find on every page.